J. T. (John Townsend) Trowbridge

A Home Idyl

And Other Poem

J. T. (John Townsend) Trowbridge

A Home Idyl
And Other Poem

ISBN/EAN: 9783744769914

Printed in Europe, USA, Canada, Australia, Japan

Cover: Foto ©Andreas Hilbeck / pixelio.de

More available books at **www.hansebooks.com**

A HOME IDYL

AND OTHER POEMS

BY

JOHN TOWNSEND TROWBRIDGE

BOSTON
HOUGHTON, MIFFLIN AND COMPANY
The Riverside Press, Cambridge
1881

CONTENTS.

A HOME IDYL.

I.

OVER the valley the storm-clouds blow,
$\qquad$ Dark and low ;
The wild air whitens with flying snow.

Through the timber two lovers ride,
$\qquad$ Side by side,
Wrapped in a shaggy buffalo-hide.

The winter has paved for their sleigh a track
$\qquad$ Over the back
Of the river rolling deep and black.

Encircled by trees which the axe has spared,
$\qquad$ In a bared
White space by the bank is their home prepared.

There Love in the wilderness far aloof
   Wove the roof :
Boughs and bark are the warp and woof.

A small rude hut amid stumps and knolls, —
   Cabin of poles,
With sticks and clay for the chinks and holes.

To that lonely door his bride he brings :
   Back it swings :
The fire is kindled, the kettle sings.

Though wooden platter and pewter plate
   Indicate
Lowly station and small estate ;

And happy they if their little hoard
   Will afford
Daily bread for that rough-hewn board ;

Though the snow, whirled round their cabin, sifts
   Through the rifts,
And up to the window climb the drifts, —

Let the forest roar and the tempest blow !
      Drive the snow !
In the heart of the hut is a heavenly glow.

Love that is mighty and Hope that is great,
      Consecrate
Wooden platter and pewter plate.

Not to mansions where abide
      Wealth and pride,
Comes ever a happier Christmas-tíde.

In the privacy of their safe retreat
      It is sweet
To hear the rush of the whirlwind's feet ;

To hear the tempest's whistling lash
      Smite the sash,
And the mighty hemlocks howl and clash.

II.

Far from the city, its life and din,
> Friends and kin,
Is the fresh new world which they begin.

In and about with busy feet,
> Light and fleet,
She keeps his cabin cozy and neat.

With shouldered axe I see him go
> Through the snow,
To clear the land for harrow and hoe.

Over his roof-tree curls the smoke,
> While the stroke
Of his axe resounds on ash and oak.

From the log at his feet, to left and right,
> Fly the bright
Splintered chips in the wintry light.

A HOME IDYL.

When the warm days come in early spring,
   She will bring
Her work to the woods and sew and sing.

'T is pleasant to feel her watching near,
   Joy to hear
Her voice in the woodland, high and clear !

Together they talk in the new-fallen tree,
   And foresee
The work of their hands in the days to be.

Where the beech comes crashing down, and the lithe
   Branches writhe,
He will turn the furrow and swing the scythe.

A rose by the doorway she will set,
   Nor forget
Pansies and pinks and mignonette.

He will burn the clearing and plant the corn ;
   She will adorn
Their house for him and their babe unborn.

-

III.

Swiftly ever, without a sound,
                    Earth goes round,
Air and ocean and solid ground.

Swiftly for them as for you and me,
                    Till they see
What they foresaw in the fallen tree.

Before their door in the summer morn,
                    Waves the corn.
'T is Christmas again, and a babe is born.

Not for the glories of wealth and art,
                    Would they part
With that small treasure of home and heart.

Dear Heaven! what springs of bliss are stirred,
                    When is heard
Its laugh or its first low lisping word!

A flower let fall by the Infinite .
Love has lit
In their path, and brought God's peace with it.

IV.

The world goes round, and year by year
Still appear
Children that add to the household cheer.

Now a daughter and now a son,
One by one
They are cradled, they creep, they walk, they run.

Sons and daughters, until behold !
Young and old,
A Jacob's-ladder with steps of gold !

A ladder of little heads ! each fair
Head a stair
For the angels that visit the parent pair.

V.

Blessèd be childhood!   Even its chains
                    Are our gains!
Welcome and blessèd, with all the pains,

Losses, and upward vanishings
                    Of light wings, —
With all the sorrow and toil it brings,

All burdens that ever those small feet bore
                    To our door, —
Blessèd and welcome for evermore!

VI.

What new delight, when over their toys
                    Girls and boys
In the Christmas dawn make a joyous noise!

Floor-boards clatter and roof-boards ring,
> When they spring
To the chimney-nook where the stockings swing.

What glee, whenever with wild applause
> One withdraws
Some wonderful gift of Santa Claus !

Let the happy little ones shout and play
> All the day !
But the hearts of the parents, where are they ?

No new-made home in the woods, but, lo !
> Swift or slow,
The same griefs follow, the same weeds grow.

To the virgin wilderness, toward the far
> Evening star,
Though we flee, there the wind-blown evils are.

The lovers had dreamed of a home without
> Pain and doubt ;
But Sorrow and Death have found them out.

The loveliest child of their love is laid
In the shade
Of the lonely pines, more lonely made

By the little grave where the vague winds blow,
And the snow
Curves mockingly over the mound below.

Let the children all the Christmas Day
Shout and play !
But the hearts of the parents turn away,

By tenderly mournful thoughts subdued,
To the rude,
Low grave in the vast gray solitude.

VII.

The world goes round with its sorrow and sin :
Now begin
The boys to plow and the girls to spin.

Gone long ago the hut of poles,
     Stumps and knolls :
A frame-house now is the shelter of souls.

By the river are farms all up and down,
     And the crown
Of its steeples shows the neighboring town.

There, market and mill for the farmer's crops,
     Schools and shops,
And white spires over the orchard-tops.

No more, to the terror of flocks and fowls,
     Hoot the owls
In the woods near by, nor the gaunt wolf howls.

Where the antlered buck on the tender boughs
     Used to browse,
Sheep come to shed and the cattle house.

Where the panther pounced on the passing fawn,
     Lies the lawn
With its untracked dew in the chill gray dawn.

Highways are braided and swamps reclaimed ;
Towns are named ;
Life is softened, manners are tamed.

For youthful culture and social grace
Soon replace
The first rude life of a pioneer race ;

And men are polished, through act and speech,
Each by each,
As pebbles are smoothed on the rolling beach.

VIII.

The farmer has hands both strong and skilled,
Fair fields tilled,
A house well kept and big barns filled.

In the porch at sunrise he will stand,
Flushed and tanned,
And view well pleased his prosperous land.

Crib and stable and pear-shaped stacks,
   Stalls and racks,
Have come in the track of the fire and axe.

Cider in cask and fruit in bin
   Are laid in
For the gloomy months that will soon begin.

Sons and daughters, a gathering throng,
   Fair and strong,
Fill the old house with life and song.

With threshing and spinning, wheat and wool,
   House and school,
Heads are busy and hands are full.

Then spelling-matches and evening calls,
   Country balls,
And sleighing-parties when the snow falls.

IX.

Foot-prints of some shy lover show,
                    Where they go
From village to farm, in the morning snow.

The farmer, florid and well-to-do,
                    Blusters, "Who
Is that bashful boy comes here to woo?"

With burning blushes and down-dropt eyes,
                    Nellie tries
To tell her trouble, but only cries.

The simple secret which poor Nell
                    Cannot tell,
The anxious mother interprets well;

And out of a wise and tender heart
                    Takes the part
Of her child with gentle, persuasive art.

" Somebody once came wooing me,
        Shy as he !
They may be poor, but so were we.

" ' No matter for wealth and grand display,'
        You would say :
' We can be happy ! ' Then why can't they ?

" We are proud, who were humble then ; but, oh !
        High or low,
Happier days we shall never know ! "

" Pooh, pooh ! well, well ! " He yields assent,
        But must vent
His grudging fatherly discontent,

That she, their child, so jealously reared,
        So endeared
By all they have borne for her, hoped and feared,

From them and their love should turn away,
        To obey
The same old law, in the same old way,

And, placing her hand in the hand of a man,
Work and plan,
Beginning the world as they began.

X.

He yields assent: the bright heaven clears
As she hears;
The red dawn breaks through her doubts and fears.

The days bring signs of a coming change:
What is the strange
New raiment the busy hands arrange?

The patterns they shape and the seams they sew?
In the glow
Of the clear dusk, over the rosy snow,

The lover comes to the farmer's door;
Shy no more,
Shy and abashed, as heretofore,

But manly of mien and open-browed,
>> Happy and proud
That his love is approved and his suit allowed.

For the father, who frowned, at last has smiled,
>> Reconciled,
On the modest youth who has won his child.

"Right sort of chap; I like his way!
>> What d' ye say?
We 'll have him at dinner Christmas Day."

XI.

A wild white world lies all around,
>> Winter-bound;
River and roof and tree and ground.

And the windows are all, at Christmas-time,
>> Thick with rime.
But the poultry is fat and the cider prime.

2

The thankful mother brings forth her best
For their guest ;
And the farmer is merry with tale and jest.

Ruby jellies in autumn stored
Crown the board ;
The goose is carved and the cider poured.

The house shows never in all the year
Better cheer,
For guest more honored or friend more dear.

Here the doctor has sat, and as he quaffed,
Praised the draught ;
At those old stories the parson has laughed.

And there with his host by the fire, the great
Magistrate
Has puffed, in familiar tête-à-tête.

The daughter listens, and glad is she,
Glad to see
Father and lover so well agree.

She listens and watches with joy and pride,
When beside
The glorious chimney, glowing wide,

They bask in the blaze of the bounteous oak,
Bask and smoke,
And the young man laughs at the elder's joke.

Lover's laughter that will not fail,
Though the tale
Be sometimes dull, or the joke be stale.

He will laugh and jest, or in graver mood
Hearken to good
Sagacious counsel, as young men should.

He reasons well ; and his wit is found
Sweet and sound ;
He can pass opinion and stand his ground.

Feats of strength and of foolery, too,
He can do,
When he joins in the games of the younger crew.

He opens his watch for the boys to see,
      On his knee;
And sings them a merry song, may be.

She shares his triumph, and thrilled to tears
      Overhears
Words meant for only the mother's ears.

"Well, yes," says the farmer, all aglow,
      Speaking low;
"As likely a fellow as any I know!"

To her pleased fancy the sweetest word
      Ever heard—
His praise of the man her love preferred!

And well may parent and child rejoice,
      When the voice
Of prudence approves the young heart's choice!

XII.

In spring the lovers pass elate
           Through the gate
With golden hinges and bolts of fate.

The gate swings open; the gate is passed;
           And at last,
For evil or good, the bolts are fast.

She may bid farewell, or linger still;
           And at will
Her feet may often recross the sill,

And tread again the familiar floor;
           Yet a door
Has closed behind her for evermore.

XIII.

'T is the exodus of youth begun ;
   One by one,
Now a daughter and now a son,

They are wooed, they woo, they pass elate
   Through the gate
With golden hinges and bolts of fate.

Some fall by the way : alas, for those
   Shall unclose
The door of the Darkness no man knows !

Two ways forever the house of breath
   Openeth,
The way of life and the way of death.

Once, may be twice, a maid shall ride,
   Now a bride,
Now in a pale robe by no man's side.

Two phantoms, traced upon every wall,
        Wait for all,
A shining bridal, a low black pall.

Though blessed the dwellers and charmed the spot,
        Palace or cot,
No home is exempt from the common lot.

XIV.

Laurels in life's first summer glow
        Rarely grow;
But honors thicken on heads of snow.

There is a lustre of swords and shields,
        Well-fought fields;
The power the statesman or patriot wields;

The glory that gleams from righted wrongs,
        Or belongs
To the prophet's words or the poet's songs, —

High thoughts that shine like the Pleiades
Over seas !
But worthy of worship, even with these,

Is the fame of an honest citizen,
Now and then ;
The good opinion of plain good men.

The farmer, solid and dignified,
Through the wide,
Fair valley on many affairs shall ride :

Through highway and by-way, country and town,
Up and down,
He shall ride in the light of his own renown.

In the halls of state, with outstretched hand,
He shall stand,
And counsel the Solons of the land.

Neighbors, wearying of the law's
Quirks and flaws,
To his good sense submit their cause.

Their cause with wary, impartial eye
He will try,
And many a snarl of the law untie.

If simple and upright men there be,
Such is he :
A life like a broad, green, sheltering tree,

For shade in the wayside heat and dust :
·All men trust
His virtue, and know his judgments just.

XV.

Not all the honors that come with age
Can assuage
The pains of its long late pilgrimage.

The world's fair offerings, great and small,
What are they all,
When the heart has losses and griefs befall ?

One by one to the parents came
> Babes to name :
One by one they have passed the same.

Hither and thither, each to his own,
> All have flown,
Like birds from the nest when their wings have grown.

‘

Beginning again the same old strife ;
> Husband and wife
Twisting the strands of the cord of life ;

Weaving ever the endless chain,
> Pleasure and pain,
The gladness of action, the joy of gain.

Hither and thither, over the zone,
> All have flown,
Like thistle-down by the four winds blown.

One has power, and one has wealth
> ,Got by stealth :
Happiest they who have hope and health.

Into the farther and wilder West
   Some have pressed ;
Some are weary, and some are at rest.

Hither and thither, like seed that is sown,
   Each to his own !
What pangs of parting these doors have known !

The tears of the young who go their way,
   Last a day ;
But the grief is long of the old who stay.

Within these gates, where they have been left,
   Long bereft,
With fond ties broken and old hearts cleft,

They have stood, and gazing across the snow,
   Felt the woe
Of seeing the last of their children go.

Now all are scattered, like leaves that are strewn :
   Through the lone,
Forsaken boughs let the wild winds moan !

XVI.

But new life comes as the old life goes,
    Life yet glows !
In children's children the fresh tide flows.

The heart of the homestead warms to the core,
    When once more
Little feet patter on path and floor. .

In the best-wrought life there is still a reft,
    Something left
Forever unfinished, a broken weft.

But merciful Nature makes amends,
    When she sends
Youth, that takes up our raveled ends,

Our hopes, our loves, that they be not quite
    Lost to sight,
But leave behind us a fringe of light.

XVII.

Age is a garden of faded flowers,
                    Ruined bowers,
Peopled by cares and failing powers ;

Where Pain with his crutch and lonely Grief
                    Grope with brief,
Slow steps over withered stalk and leaf.

But the love of children is like some rare
                    Heavenly air,
That makes long Indian summer there ;

A youth in age, when the skies yet glow,
                    Soft winds blow,
And hearts keep glad under locks of snow.

XVIII.

So the old couple long abide
            In the wide
Old-fashioned house by the river side.

Is life but a pool of trouble and sin?
            Theirs has been
As a cup to pour Heaven's mercies in!

Happy are they who, calm and chaste,
            Freely taste
Each day's brimmed measure, nor haste nor waste;

Who love not the world too well, nor hate;
            But await
With faith the coming of unknown fate;

Pleased amid simple sights and sounds,
            In these bounds
Of a life which Infinite Life surrounds!

With doubt and bitterness and ennui,
> Life can be
But an ashy fruit by the heart's Dead Sea.

To cheerful endeavor and sacrifice
> It shall rise
Each day forever a new surprise.

XIX.

Now daughters and sons, from far and near,
> Reappear,
And the day of all golden days is here.

Experienced matrons, world-wise men
> Come again:
They are seven to-day who once were ten.

Are these the children who left your door?
> Look once more!
O mother! are these the babes you bore?

Where 's she, who was once so fresh and fair?
　　　　Nell is there,
A grandmother now with silvered hair !

And is this the lover who came to woo?
　　　　Now he too
Is solid and florid and well-to-do.

One has acres and railroad shares,
　　　　But no heirs ;
One, a house full of children and poor man's cares.

But all distinction in life to-day
　　　　Falls away,
Like costume dropped with the parts they play.

Here all, whatever success they claim,
　　　　Rank the same ;
And the half-forgotten household name,

As in old days, rings out again :
　　　　Now as then
It is *Tom* and *Nellie* and *Sallie* and *Ben*.

All smiles, all tears, through a shining haze,
In a maze
Of wonder and joy, the old folks gaze.

Three generations around them stand,
Hand in hand,
As the petals of some vast flower expand.

Sons, daughters, husbands and wives inclose
Younger rows,
Children's children, and children of those:

Whose children may yet with a living girth
Circle earth:
Oh infinite marvel of life and birth!

This is the crowning hour that cheers
Failing years,
This is the solace of many tears.

Past sorrows, viewed from that sunset height,
Fade from sight,
Or glimmer far off in softened light.

3

Remembered mercies and joys increase,
            Trials cease,
And all is blessedness, all is peace.

XX.

The world goes round with its hopes and fears,
            Joys and tears :
'T is Christmas again, in the latter years.

To the white grave-yard, through the snow,
            Dark and slow,
I see a solemn procession go.

Where first he hollowed the mold and piled,
            In the wild
Great woods, the mound of his little child, —

Softly muffled to sight and tread,
            Lies outspread
The field of the unremembering dead.

Neighbor with neighbor sleeps below,
    Foe with foe,
Their quarrels forgotten long ago.

Once more, with its burden that goes not back,
    Moves the black
Far-followed hearse, on its frequent track,

To the voiceless bourne of all the vast
    Peopled past :
Thither, from all life's ways at last,

From all its raptures and all its woes,
    Thither goes
The old patriarch to his long repose.

Close by where children and wife are laid,
    Leans a spade
By the dark heaped earth of a grave just made.

The heavily-laden firs, snow-crowned,
    Droop around,
With tent-like branches that sweep the ground.

The slow procession makes halt amid
Slabs half-hid,
Snow-mantled tablet and pyramid ;

Whose fairest marble looks poor and pale
By the frail
And careless sculpture of snow and gale.

The trestles are set, the bier they place
In mid-space,
And lift the lid from the upturned face, —

Still smiling, as when the soul took flight
In a bright
Last vision of sudden angelic light.

Where, scheming world, are your triumphs now ?
All things bow
Before Death's pallid and awful brow.

Hearts are humbled and heads are bare,
While the prayer
Is wafted far on the wintry air.

Friends gather and pass, and tears are shed
Over the dead:
They gather and pass with reverent tread.

They have looked their last and turned away;
From the day
Veil forever the face of clay!

The glory that gilds this wondrous ball,
Lighting all,
No more forever on him shall fall.

The throng moves outward; clangs the great
Iron gate:
All's ended: lonely and desolate

Appears, in the white and silent ground,
One dark mound;
And the world goes round, the world goes round.

OLD ROBIN.

SELL old Robin, do you say? Well, I reckon not to-
     day!
I have let you have your way with the land,
With the meadows and the fallows, draining swamps and
     filling hollows,
And you 're mighty deep, Dan Alvord! but the sea itself
     has shallows,
And there *are* things that you *don't* understand.

You are not so green, of course, as to feed a worn-out
     horse,
Out of pity or remorse, very long!
But as sure as I am master of a shed and bit of pasture,
Not for all the wealth, I warn you, of a Vanderbilt or
     Astor,
Will I do old Robin there such a wrong.

He *is* old and lame, alas! Don't disturb him as you
    pass!
Let him lie there on the grass, while he may,
And enjoy the summer weather, free forever from his
    tether.
Sober veteran as you see him, we were young and gay
    together:
It was I who rode him first — ah, the day!

I was just a little chap, in first pantaloons and cap,
And I left my mother's lap, at the door;
And the reins hung loose and idle, as we let him prance
    and sidle, —
For my father walked beside me with his hand upon the
    bridle:
Yearling colt and boy of five, hardly more.

See him start and prick his ears! see how knowingly he
    leers!
I believe he overhears every word,
And once more, it may be, fancies that he carries me
    and prances,

While my mother from the doorway follows us with
    happy glances.
You may laugh, but — well, of course, it 's absurd !

Poor old Robin ! does he know how I used to cling and
    crow,
As I rode him to and fro and around ?
Every day as we grew older, he grew gentler, I grew
    bolder,
Till, a hand upon the bridle and a touch upon his
    shoulder,
I could vault into my seat at a bound.

Ah, the nag you so disdain, with his scanty tail and
    mane,
And that ridge-pole to shed rain, called a back,
Then was taper-limbed and glossy, — so superb a creat-
    ure was he !
And he arched his neck, so graceful, and he tossed his
    tail, so saucy,
Like a proudly waving plume long and black !

He was light of hoof and fleet, I was supple, firm in
    seat,

And no sort of thing with feet, anywhere
In the country, could come nigh us; scarce the swallows
    could outfly us;
But the planet spun beneath us, and the sky went whiz-
    zing by us,
In the hurricane we made of the air.

Then I rode away to school in the mornings fresh and
    cool;
Till, one day, beside the pool where he drank,
Leaning on my handsome trotter, glancing up across the
    water
To the judge's terraced orchard, there I saw the judge's
    daughter,
In a frame of sunny boughs on the bank.

Looking down on horse and boy, smiling down, so sweet
    and coy,
That I thrilled with bashful joy, when she said, —
Voice as sweet as a canary's, — "Would you like to get
    some cherries?
You are welcome as the birds are; there are nice ones
    on this terrace;
These are white-hearts in the tree overhead."

Was it Robin more than I, that had pleased her girlish
    eye

As she saw us prancing by? half I fear!

Off she ran, but not a great way: white-hearts, black-
    hearts, sweethearts straightway!

Boy and horse were soon familiar with the hospitable
    gateway,

And a happy fool was I — for a year.

Lord forgive an only child! All the blessings on me
    piled

Had but helped to make me wild and perverse.

What is there in honest horses that should lead to
    vicious courses?

Racing, betting, idling, tippling, wasted soon my best
    resources:

Small beginnings led to more — and to worse.

Father? happy in his grave! Praying mothers cannot
    save;—

Mine? a flatterer and a slave to her son!

Often Mary urged and pleaded, and the good judge in-
    terceded,

Counseled, blamed, insisted, threatened : tears and
    threats were all unheeded,
And I answered him in wrath : it was done !

Vainly Mary sobbed and clung ; in a fury out I flung,
To old Robin's back I sprung, and away !
No repentance, no compassion ; on I plunged in head-
    long fashion,
In a night of rain and tempest, with a fierce, despairing
    passion, —
Through the blind and raving gusts, mad as they.

Bad to worse was now my game : my poor mother, still
    the same,
Tried to shield me, to reclaim — did her best.
Creditors began to clamor ; I could only lie and stam-
    mer ;
All we had was pledged for payment, all was sold be-
    neath the hammer —
My old Robin there, along with the rest.

Laughing, jeering, I stood by, with a devil in my eye,
Watching those who came to buy : what was done

I had then no power to alter; I looked on and would
    not falter,
Till the last man had departed, leading Robin by the
    halter;
Then I flew into the loft for my gun.

I would shoot him! no, I said, I would kill myself in-
    stead!
To a lonely wood I fled, on a hill.
Hating Heaven and all its mercies for my follies and re-
    verses,
There I plunged in self-abasement, there I burrowed in
    self-curses;
But the dying I put off — as men will.

As I wandered back at night, something, far off, caught
    my sight,
Dark against the western light, in the lane;
Coming to the bars to meet me — some illusion sent to
    cheat me!
No, 'twas Robin, my own Robin, dancing, whinnying to
    greet me!
With a small white billet sewed to his mane.

The small missive I unstrung — on old Robin's neck I
    hung,

There I cried and there I clung! while I read,

In a hand I knew was Mary's — "One whose kindness
    never varies

Sends this gift:" no name was written, but a painted
    bunch of cherries

On the dainty little note smiled instead.

There he lies now! lank and lame, stiff of limb and
    gaunt of frame,

But to her and me the same dear old boy!

Never steed, I think, was fairer! Still I see him the
    proud bearer

Of my pardon and salvation; and he yet shall be a
    sharer —

As a poor dumb beast may share — in my joy.

It is strange that by the time, I, a man, am in my prime,

He is guilty of the crime of old age!

But no sort of circumvention can deprive him of his pen-
    sion :

He shall have his rack and pasture, with a little kind at-
tention,
And some years of comfort yet, I 'll engage.

By long service and good will he has earned them, and
he still
Has a humble place to fill, as you know.
Now my little shavers ride him, sometimes two or three
astride him;
Mary watches from the doorway while I lead or walk be-
side him; —
But his dancing all was done long ago.

See that merry, toddling lass tripping to and fro, to pass
Little handfuls of green grass, which he chews,
And the two small urchins trying to climb up and ride
him lying;
And, hard-hearted as you are, Dan, — eh? you don't
say! you are crying?
Well, an old horse, after all, has his use!

PLEASANT STREET.

'T is Pleasant, indeed,
As the letters read
On the guideboard at the crossing.
Over the street
The branches meet,
Gently swaying and tossing.

Through its leafy crown
The sun strikes down
In wavering flakes and flashes,
As winding it goes
Betwixt tall rows
Of maples and elms and ashes.

There, high aloof
In the gilded roof,
Are the phœbe and vireo winging

Their fitful flight
In the flickering light;
The hangbird's basket swinging.

By many a great
And small estate,
And orchard cool and pleasant,
And croquet-ground,
The way sweeps round,
In many a curve and crescent.

In crescents and curves
It sways and swerves,
Like the flow of a stately river.
On carriage and span,
On maiden and man,
The dappling sunbeams quiver.

It winds between
Broad slopes of the green
Wood-mantled and shaggy highland,
And shores that rise
From the lake, which lies
Below, with its one fair island.

The long days dawn
Over lake and lawn,
And set on the hills ; and at even
Above it beam
All the lights that gleam
In the starry streets of heaven.

But not for these,
Lake, lawns and trees,
And gardens gay in their season, —
Its praise I sing
For a sweeter thing,
And a far more human reason.

Children I meet
In house and street,
Pretty maids and happy mothers,
All fair to see ;
But one to me
More beautiful than all others !

One whose pure face,
With its glancing grace,
Makes every one her lover ;

Charming the sight
With a sweeter light
Than falls from the boughs above her.

Though on each side
Are the homes of pride,
And of beauty, — here and there one, —
The dearest of all,
Though simple and small,
Is the dwelling of my fair one.

You will marvel that such
A gay sprite so much
Of a grave man's life engages,
And smile when I
Confess with a sigh
The difference in our ages.

Must love depart
With our youth, and the heart,
As we grow in years, become colder?
My love is but four,
While I am twoscore,
And may be a trifle older.

With her smile and her glance,
And her curls that dance,
No one could ever resist her.
If anywhere
There 's another so fair,
Why, that must be her sister.

With screams of glee
At the sight of me,
Together forth they sally
From under the boughs
That screen the house
That stands beside the valley.

It is scenes like these,
As they clasp my knees
And clamor for kiss and present,
That still must make
Our street by the lake
More pleasant — oh, most pleasant !

Ride merrily past,
Glide smoothly and fast,
O throngs of wealth and of pleasure !

While sober and slow
On foot I go,
Enjoying my humble leisure.

O World, before
My lowly door
Daily coming and going;
O tide of life,
O stream of strife,
Forever ebbing and flowing!

By the show and the shine
No eye can divine
If you be fair or hateful;
I only know,
As you come and go,
That I am glad and grateful.

So here, well back
From the shaded track,
By the curve of its greenest crescent,
To-day I swing
In my hammock, and sing
The praise of the street named *Pleasant.*

MENOTOMY LAKE.[1]

THERE 's nothing so sweet as a morning in May,
　And what is so fair as the gleam of glad water?
Spring leaps from the brow of old Winter to-day,
　Full-formed, like the fabled Olympian's daughter.

A breath out of heaven came down in the night,
　Dispelling the gloom of the sullen northeasters;
The air is all balm, and the lake is as bright
　As some bird in brave plumage that ripples and glis-
　　ters.

The enchantment is broken which bound her so long,
　And Beauty, that slumbered, awakes and remembers;
Love bursts into being, joy breaks into song,
　In a glory of blossoms life flames from its embers.

[1] The Indian name for Arlington Lake, or Spy Pond.

I row by steep woodlands, I rest on my oars
Under banks deep-embroidered with grass and young
clover ;
Far round, in and out, wind the beautiful shores, —
The lake in the midst, with the blue heavens over.

The world in its mirror hangs dreamily bright ;
The patriarch clouds in curled raiment, that lazily
Lift their bare foreheads in dazzling white light,
In that deep under-sky glimmer softly and hazily.

Far over the trees, or in glimpses between,
Peer the steeples and half-hidden roofs of the village.
Here lie the broad slopes in their loveliest green ;
There, crested with orchards, or checkered with tillage.

There the pines, tall and black, in the blue morning air ;
The warehouse of ice, a vast windowless castle ;
The ash and the sycamore, shadeless and bare ;
The elm-boughs in blossom, the willows in tassel.

In golden effulgence of leafage and blooms,
Far along, overleaning, the sunshiny willows

Advance like a surge from the grove's deeper glooms, —
  The first breaking swell of the summer's green bil-
      lows.

Scarce a tint upon hornbeam or sumach appears,
  The arrowhead tarries, the lily still lingers;
But the flag-leaves are piercing the wave with their spears,
  And the fern is unfolding its infantile fingers.

Down through the dark evergreens slants the mild light:
  I know every cove, every moist indentation,
Where mosses and violets ever invite
  To some still unexperienced, fresh exploration.

The mud-turtle, sunning his shield on a log,
  Slides off with a splash as my paddle approaches;
Beside the green island I silence the frog,
  In warm, sunny shallows I startle the roaches.

I glide under branches where rank above rank
  From the lake grow the trees, bending over its bo-
      som;

Or lie in my boat on some flower-starred bank,
  And drink in delight from each bird-song and blossom.

Above me the robins are building their nest;
  The finches are here, — singing throats by the dozen;
The cat-bird, complaining, or mocking the rest;
  The wing-spotted blackbird, sweet bobolink's cousin.

With rapture I watch, as I loiter beneath,
  The small silken tufts on the boughs of the beeches,
Each leaf-cluster parting its delicate sheath,
  As it gropingly, yearningly opens and reaches;

Like soft-wingèd things coming forth from their shrouds.
  The bees have forsaken the maples' red flowers
And gone to the willows, whose luminous clouds
  Drop incense and gold in impalpable showers.

The bee-peopled odorous boughs overhead,
  With fragrance and murmur the senses delighting;
The lake-side, gold-laced with the pollen they shed
  At the touch of a breeze or a small bird alighting;

The myriad tremulous pendants that stream
   From the hair of the birches, — O group of slim graces,
That see in the water your silver limbs gleam,
   And lean undismayed over infinite spaces ! —

The bold dandelions embossing the grass ;
   On upland and terrace the fruit-gardens blooming ; ·
The wavering, winged, happy creatures that pass, —
   Pale butterflies flitting, and bumble-bees booming ;

The crowing of cocks and the bellow of kine ;
   Light, color, and all the delirious lyrical
Bursts of bird-voices ; life filled with new wine, —
   Every motion and change in this beautiful miracle,

Springtime and Maytime, — revive in my heart
   All the springs of my youth, with their sweetness and
      splendor :
O years that so softly take wing and depart !
   O perfume ! O memories pensive and tender !

As lightly I glide between island and shore,
   I seem like an exile, a wandering spirit,

Returned to the land where 't is May evermore,
  A moment revisiting, hovering near it.

Stray scents from afar, breathing faintly around,
  Are something I 've known in another existence;
As I pause, as I listen, each image, each sound,
  Is softened by glamour, or mellowed by distance.

From the hill-side, no longer discordant or harsh,
  Comes the cry of the peacock, the jubilant cackle;
And sweetly, how sweetly, by meadow and marsh,
  Sounds the musical jargon of blue-jay and grackle!

O Earth! till I find more of heaven than this,
  I will cling to your bosom with perfect contentment.
O water! O light! sky-enfolded abyss!
  I yield to the spell of your wondrous enchantment.

I drift on the dream of a lake in my boat;
  With my oar-beat two pinion-like shadows keep meas-
      ure;
I poise and gaze down through the depths as I float,
  Seraphic, sustained between azure and azure.

I pause in a rift, by the edge of the world,

    That divides the blue gulfs of a double creation ;

Till, lo, the illusion is shattered and whirled

    In a thousand bright rings by my skiff's oscillation !

THE INDIAN CAMP.

OUT from the Northern forest, dim and vast;
    Out from the mystéry
Of yet more shadowy times, a pathless past,
    Untracked by History;

Strangely he comes into our commonplace,
    Prosaic present;
And, like a faded star beside the bay's
    Silvery crescent,

Upon the curved shore of the shining lake
    His tent he pitches —
A modern chief, in white man's wide-awake
    And Christian breeches.

Reckless of title-deeds and forms of law,
    He freely chooses

Whatever slope or wood-side suits his squaw
    And lithe papooses.

Why not ?   The owners of the land were red,
    Holding dominion
Wherever ranged the foot of beast or spread
    The eagle's pinion ;

And privileged, until they welcomed here
    Their fair-faced brother,
To hunt at will, sometimes the bear and deer,
    Sometimes each other.

How often to this lake, down yonder dark
    And sinuous river,
The painted warriors sailed, in fleets of bark,
    With bow and quiver !

This lank-haired chieftain is their child, and heir
    To a great nation,
And well might fix, you fancy, anywhere
    His habitation.

Has he too come to hunt the bear and deer,
To trap the otter?
Alas! there's no such creature stirring here,
On land or water.

To have a little traffic with the town,
Once more he chooses
The ancient camping-place, and brings his brown
Squaw and papooses.

No tent was here in yester-evening's hush;
But the day, dawning,
Transfigures with a faint, a roseate flush,
His dingy awning.

The camp-smoke curling in the misty light,
And canvas slanting
To the green earth, all this is something quite
Fresh and enchanting;

Viewed not too closely, lest the glancing wings,
The iridescent
Soft colors of romance, give place to things
Not quite so pleasant.

The gossamers glistening on the dewy turf ;
    The lisp and tinkle
Of flashing foam-bells, where the placid surf
    Breaks on the shingle ;

The shimmering birches by the rippling cove ;
    A fresh breeze bringing
The fragrance of the pines, and in the grove
    The thrushes singing,

Make the day sweet.   But other sight and sound
    And odor fill it,
You find, as you approach their camping-ground
    And reeking skillet.

The ill-fed curs rush out with wolfish bark ;
    And, staring at you,
A slim young girl leaps up, smooth-limbed and dark
    As a bronze statue.

A bare papoose about the camp-fire poles
    Toddles at random ;
And on the ground there, by the blazing coals,
    Sits the old grandam.

Wrinkled and lean, her skirt a matted rag,
In plaited collar
Of beads and hedghog quills, the smoke-dried hag
Squats in her squalor,

Dressing a marmot which the boys have shot;
Which done, she seizes
With tawny claws, and drops into the pot,
The raw, red pieces.

The chief meanwhile has in some mischief found
A howling urchin,
Who knows too well, alas! that he is bound
To have a birching.

The stoic of the woods, stern and unmoved,
Lays the light lash on,
Tickling the lively ankles in approved
Fatherly fashion.

The boy slinks off, a wiser boy, indeed —
Wiser and sorrier.
And is this he, the chief of whom we read,
The Indian warrior?

Where hangs his tomahawk? the scalps of tall
　　Braves struck in battle?
Why, bless you, sir, his band is not at all
　　That kind of cattle!

In ceasing to be savages, they chose
　　To put away things
That suit the savage: even those hickory bows
　　Are merely playthings.

For common use he rather likes, I think,
　　The white man's rifle,
Hatchet, and blanket; and of white man's drink,
　　I fear, a trifle.

With neighbors' scalp-locks, and such bagatelles,
　　He never meddles.
Bows, baskets, and I hardly know what else,
　　He makes and peddles.

Quite civilized, you see.　Is he aware
　　Of his beatitude?
5

Does he, for all the white man's love and care,
　　Feel proper gratitude?

Feathers and war-paint he no more enjoys;
　　But he is prouder
Of long-tailed coat, and boots, and corduroys,
　　And white man's powder.

And he can trade his mink and musquash skins,
　　Baskets of wicker,
For white man's trinkets; bows and moccasins
　　For white man's liquor.

His Manitou is passing, with each strange,
　　Wild superstition:
He has the Indian agent for a change,
　　And Indian mission.

He owns his cabin and potato patch,
　　And farms a little.
Industrious? Quite, when there are fish to catch,
　　Or shafts to whittle.

Though all about him, like a rising deep,
    Flows the white nation,
He has — and while it pleases us may keep —
    His Reservation.

Placed with his tribe in such a paradise,
    'T is past believing
That they should still be given to petty vice,
    Treachery, and thieving.

Incentives to renounce their Indian tricks
    Are surely ample,
With white man's piety and politics
    For their example.

But are they happier now than when, some night,
    The chosen quotas
Of tufted warriors sallied forth to fight
    The fierce Dakotas?

Still under that sedate, impassive port,
    That dull demeanor,
A spirit waits, a demon sleeps — in short,
    The same red sinner!

Within those inky pools, his eyes, I see
    Revenge and pillage,
The midnight massacre that yet may be,
    The blazing village.

When will he mend his wicked ways, indeed,
    Kill more humanely —
Depart, and leave to us the lands we need?
    To put it plainly.

Yet in our dealings with his race, in crimes
    Of war and ravage,
Who is the Christian, one might ask sometimes,
    And who the savage?

His traits are ours, seen in a dusky glass,
    And but remind us
Of heathenism we hardly yet, alas!
    Have left behind us.

Is right for white race wrong for black and red?
    A man or woman,
What hue soever, after all that's said,
    Is simply human.

Viewed from the smoke and misery of his dim
        Civilization,
How seems, I'd like to ask — how seems to him
        The proud Caucasian?

I shape the question as he saunters nigh,
        But shame to ask it.
We turn to price his wares instead, and buy,
        Perhaps, a basket.

But this is strange!   A man without pretense
        Of wit or reading,
Where did he get that calm intelligence,
        That plain good-breeding?

With him long patience, fortitude unspent,
        Untaught sagacity:
Culture with us, the curse of discontent,
        Pride, and rapacity.

Something we gain of him and bear away
        Beside our purchase.
We look awhile upon the quivering bay
        And shimmering birches —

The young squaw bearing up from the canoes
Some heavy lading ;
Along the beach a picturesque papoose
Splashing and wading ;

The withered crone, the camp-smoke's slow ascent,
The puffs that blind her ;
The girl, her silhouette on the sun-lit tent
Shadowed behind her ;

The stalwart brave, watching his burdened wife,
Erect and stolid :
We look, and think with pity of a life
So poor and squalid !

Then at the cheering signal of a bell
We slowly wander
Back to the world, back to the great hotel
Looming up yonder.

AN IDYL OF HARVEST TIME.

Swift cloud, swift light, now dark, now bright, across the
    landscape played ;
And, spotted as a leopard's side in chasing sun and
    shade,
To far dim heights and purple vales ·the upland rolled
    away,
Where the soft, warm haze of summer days on all the
    distance lay.

From shorn and hoary harvest-fields to barn and brist-
    ling stack,
The wagon bore its beetling loads, or clattered empty
    back ;
The leaning oxen clashed their horns and swayed along
    the road,
And the old house-dog lolled beside, in the shadow of
    the load.

The children played among the sheaves, the hawk went
    sailing over,
The yellow-bird was on the bough, the bee was on the
    clover,
While at my easel by the oak I sketched, and sketched
    in vain : —
Could I but group those harvesters, paint sunshine on
    the grain !

While everywhere, in the golden air, the soul of beauty
    swims,
It will not guide my feeble touch, nor light the hand that
    limns.
(The load moves on — that cloud is gone ! I must keep
    down the glare
Of sunshine on my stubble-land. Those boys are my
    despair !)

My fancies flit away at last, and wander like the
    gleams
Of shifting light along the hills, and drift away in
    dreams ;

Till, coming round the farm-house porch and down the
    shady lane,
A form is seen, half hid, between the stooks of shaggy
    grain.

Beside my easel, at the oak, I wait to see her pass.
'T is luncheon-time : the harvesters are resting on the
    grass.
I watch her coming to the gap, and envy Master Ben
Who meets her there, and helps to bear her basket to
    the men.

In the flushed farmer's welcoming smile, there beams a
    father's pride.
More quiet grows, more redly glows, the shy youth by
    his side :
In the soft passion of his look, and in her kind, bright
    glance,
I learn a little mystery, I read a sweet romance.

With pewter mug, and old brown jug, she laughing
    kneels : I hear
The liquid ripple of her lisp, with the gurgle of the beer.

That native grace, that charming face, those glances coy
    and sweet,
Ben, with the basket, grinning near — my grouping is
    complete !

The picture grows, the landscape flows, and heart and
    fancy burn, —
The figures start beneath my brush! (So you the rule
    may learn :
Let thought be thrilled with sympathy, right touch and
    tone to give,
And mix your colors with heart's blood, to make the
    canvas live.)

All this was half a year ago : I find the sketch to-day, —
Faulty and crude enough, no doubt, but it wafts my soul
    away !
I tack it to the wall, and lo ! despite the winter's gloom,
It makes a little spot of sun and summer in my room.

Again the swift cloud-shadow sweeps across the stooks
    of rye ;
The cricket trills, the locust shrills, the hawk goes sail-
    ing by ;

The yellow-bird is on the bough, the bee is on the
    thistle,

The quail is near — " Ha hoyt! " — I hear his almost
    human whistle !

THE OLD BURYING-GROUND.

PLUMED ranks of tall wild-cherry
 And birch surround
The half-hid, solitary
 Old burying-ground.

All the low wall is crumbled
 And overgrown,
And in the turf lies tumbled,
 Stone upon stone.

Only the school-boy, scrambling
 After his arrow
Or lost ball, — searching, trampling
 The tufts of yarrow,

Of milkweed and slim mullein, —
 The place disturbs;

Or bowed wise-woman, culling
    Her magic herbs.

No more the melancholy
    Dark trains draw near ;
The dead possess it wholly
    This many a year.

The head-stones lean, winds whistle,
    The long grass waves,
Rank grow the dock and thistle
    Over the graves ;

And all is waste, deserted,
    And drear, as though
Even the ghosts departed
    Long years ago !

The squirrels start forth and chatter
    To see me pass ;
Grasshoppers leap and patter
    In the dry grass.

I hear the drowsy drumming
Of woodpeckers,
And suddenly at my coming
The quick grouse whirs.

Untouched through all mutation
Of times and skies,
A by-gone generation
Around me lies :

Of high and low condition,
Just and unjust,
The patient and physician,
All turned to dust.

Suns, snows, drought, cold, birds, blossoms,
Visit the spot ;
Rains drench the quiet bosoms,
Which heed them not.

Under an aged willow,
The earth my bed,
A mossy mound my pillow,
I lean my head.

Babe of this mother, dying
    A fresh young bride,
That old, old man is lying
    Here by her side !

I muse : above me hovers
    A haze of dreams :
Bright maids and laughing lovers,
    Life's morning gleams ;

The past with all its passions,
    Its toils and wiles,
Its ancient follies, fashions,
    And tears and smiles ;

With thirsts and fever-rages,
    And ceaseless pains,
Hoarding as for the ages
    Its little gains !

Fair lives that bloom and wither,
    Their summer done ;
Loved forms with heart-break hither
    Borne one by one.

Wife, husband, child and mother,
Now reck no more
Which mourned on earth the other,
Or went before.

The soul, risen from its embers,
In its blest state
Perchance not even remembers
Its earthly fate ;

Nor heeds, in the duration
Of spheres sublime,
This pebble of creation,
This wave of time.

For a swift moment only
Such dreams arise ;
Then, turning from this lonely,
Tossed field, my eyes

Through clumps of whortleberry
And brier look down
Toward yonder cemetery,
And modern town,

Where still men build, and marry,
    And strive, and mourn,
And now the dark pall carry,
    And now are borne.

6

A STORY OF THE "BAREFOOT BOY."

WRITTEN FOR J. G. WHITTIER'S SEVENTIETH BIRTHDAY.

"I was once a barefoot boy." — J. G. WHITTIER.

ON Haverhill's pleasant hills there played,
  Some sixty years ago,
In turned-up trousers, tattered hat,
Patches and freckles, and all that,
  The Barefoot Boy we know.

He roamed his berry-fields content ;
  But while, from bush and brier
The nimble feet got many a scratch,
His wit, beneath its homely thatch,
  Aspired to something higher.

Over his dog-eared spelling-book,
　Or school-boy composition,
Puzzling his head with some hard sum,
Going for nuts, or gathering gum,
　He cherished his ambition.

He found the turtles' eggs, and watched
　To see the warm sun hatch 'em;
Hunted, with sling, or bow and arrow,
Or salt, to trap the unwary sparrow;
　Caught fish, or tried to catch 'em.

But more and more, to rise, to soar —
　This hope his bosom fired.
He shot his shaft, he sailed his kite,
Let out the string and watched its flight,
　And smiled, while he aspired.

"Now I've a plan — I know we can!"
　He said to Mat — another
Small shaver of the barefoot sort:
His name was Matthew; Mat, for short;
　Our barefoot's younger brother.

"What! fly?" says Mat.   "Well, not just that."
     John thought : " No, we can't fly ;
  But we can go right up," says he,
" Oh, higher than the highest tree !
     Away up in the sky ! "

"Oh do ! " says Mat ; " I 'll hold thy hat,
     And watch while thee is gone."
  For these were Quaker lads, and each
  Lisped in his pretty Quaker speech.
     " No, *that* won't do," says John.

" For thee must help ; then we can float,
     As light as any feather.
  We both can lift ; now don't thee see ?
  If thee 'll lift me while I lift thee,
     We shall go up together ! "

An autumn evening ; early dusk ;
     A few stars faintly twinkled ;
  The crickets chirped ; the chores were done ;
  'T was just the time to have some fun,
     Before the tea-bell tinkled.

They spat upon their hands, and clinched,
  Firm under-hold and upper.
"Don't lift too hard, or lift too far,"
Says Mat, "or we may hit a star,
  And not get back to supper!"

"Oh, no!" says John; "we'll only lift
  A few rods up, that's all,
To see the river and the town.
Now don't let go till we come down,
  Or we shall catch a fall!

"Hold fast to me! now; one, two, three!
  And up we go!" They jerk,
They pull and strain, but all in vain!
A bright idea, and yet, 't was plain,
  It somehow would n't work.

John gave it up; ah, many a John
  Has tried and failed, as he did!
'T was a shrewd notion, none the less,
And still, in spite of ill success,
  It somehow has succeeded.

Kind nature smiled on that wise child,
Nor could her love deny him
The large fulfillment of his plan ;
Since he who lifts his brother man
In turn is lifted by him.

He reached the starry heights of peace
Before his head was hoary ;
And now, at threescore years and ten,
The blessings of his fellow-men
Waft him a crown of glory.

RECOLLECTIONS OF "LALLA ROOKH."

READ AT THE MOORE BANQUET IN BOSTON, MAY 27, 1879.

WHEN we were farm-boys, years ago,
  I dare not tell how many, ˌ
When, strange to say, the fairest day
  Was often dark and rainy;

No work, no school, no weeds to pull,
  No picking up potatoes,
No copy-page to fill with blots,
  With little o's or great O's;

But jokes and stories in the barn
  Made quiet fun and frolic;
Draughts, fox-and-geese, and games like these,
  Quite simple and bucolic;

Naught else to do, but just to braid
    A lash, or sing and whittle,
Or go, perhaps, and set our traps,
    If it "held up" a little;

On one of those fine days, for which
    We boys were always wishing,
Too wet to sow, or plant, or hoe,
    Just right to go a fishing, —

I found, not what I went to seek,
    In the old farmhouse gable, —
Nor line, nor hook, but just a book
    That lay there on the table,

Beside my sister's candlestick
    (The wick burned to the socket);
A handy book to take to bed,
    Or carry in one's pocket.

I tipped the dainty cover back,
    With little thought of finding
Anything half so bright within
    The red morocco binding;

And let by chance my careless glance
   Range over song and story ;
When from between the magic leaves
   There streamed a sudden glory, —

As from a store of sunlit gems,
   Pellucid and prismatic, —
That edged with gleams the rough old beams,
   And filled the raftered attic.

I stopped to read ; I took no heed
   Of time or place, or whether
The window-pane was streaked with rain,
   Or bright with clearing weather.

Of chore-time or of supper-time
   I had no thought or feeling ;
If calves were bleating to be fed,
   Or hungry pigs were squealing.

The tangled web of tale and rhyme,
   Enraptured, I unraveled;
By caravan, through Hindostan,
   Toward gay Cashmere, I traveled.

Before the gate of Paradise
   I pleaded with the Peri ;
And even of queer old Fadladeen
   I somehow did not weary ;

Until a voice called out below :
   " Come, boys ! the rain is over !
It 's time to bring the cattle home !
   The lambs are in the clover ! "

My dream took flight ; but day or night,
   It came again, and lingered.
I kept the treasure in my coat,
   And many a time I fingered

Its golden leaves among the sheaves
   In the long harvest nooning ;
Or in my room, till fell the gloom,
   And low boughs let the moon in.

About me beamed another world,
   Refulgent, oriental ;
Life all aglow with poetry,
   Or sweetly sentimental.

My hands were filled with common tasks,
    My head with rare romances ;
My old straw hat was bursting out
    With light locks and bright fancies.

In field or wood, my thoughts threw off
    The old prosaic trammels ;
The sheep were grazing antelopes,
    The cows, a train of camels.

Under the shady apple-boughs,
    The book was my companion ;
And while I read, the orchard spread
    One mighty branching banyan.

To mango-trees or almond-groves
    Were changed the plums and quinces.
I was the poet, Feramorz,
    And had, of course, my Princess.

The well-curb was her canopied,
    Rich palanquin ; at twilight,
'T was her pavilion overhead,
    And not my garret skylight.

Ah, Lalla Rookh! O charmèd book!
　First love, in manhood slighted!
To-day we rarely turn the page
　In which our youth delighted.

Moore stands upon our shelves to-day,
　I fear a trifle dusty;
With Scott, beneath a cobweb wreath,
　And Byron, somewhat musty.

But though his orient cloth-of-gold
　Is hardly now the fashion,
His tender melodies will live
　While human hearts have passion.

The centuries roll; but he has left,
　Beside the ceaseless river,
Some flowers of rhyme untouched by Time,
　And songs that sing forever.

FILLING AN ORDER.

READ AT THE HOLMES BREAKFAST, BOSTON, DEC. 3, 1879.

To Nature, in her shop one day, at work compounding
    simples,
Studying fresh tints for Beauty's cheeks, or new effects in
    dimples,
An order came : she wiped in haste her fingers and un-
    folded
The scribbled scrap, put on her specs, and read it, while
    she scolded.

" From Miss Columbia !   I declare ! of all the upstart
    misses !
What will the jade be asking next ?   Now what an order
    this is !

Where's Boston ? Oh, that one-horse town out there
    beside the ocean !
She wants — of course, she always wants — another little
    notion !

"This time, three geniuses, A 1, to grace her favorite
    city :
The first a bard ; the second wise ; the third supremely
    witty ;
None of the staid and hackneyed sort, but some peculiar
    flavor,
Something unique and fresh for each, will be esteemed a
    favor !
Modest demands ! as if my hands had but to turn and
    toss over
A Poet veined with dew and fire, a Wit, and a Philoso-
    pher !

"But now let's see ! " She put aside her old, outworn
    expedients,
And in a quite unusual way began to mix ingredients, —
Some in the fierce retort distilled, some pounded by the
    pestle, —

And set the simmering souls to steep, each in its glowing
  vessel.

In each, by turns, she poured, she stirred, she skimmed
  the shining liquor,

Threw laughter in, to make it thin, or thought, to make
  it thicker.

But when she came to choose the clay, she found, to her
  vexation,

That, with a stock on hand to fill an order for a nation,

Of that more finely tempered stuff, electric and ethereal,

Of which a genius must be formed, she had but scant
  material —

For three ? For one ! What should be done ? A bright
  idea struck her ;

Her old witch-eyes began to shine, her mouth began to
  pucker.

Says she, " The fault, I 'm well aware, with genius is the
  presence

Of altogether too much clay, with quite too little es-
  sence,

And sluggish atoms that obstruct the spiritual solution ;

So now, instead of spoiling these by over-much dilution,

With their fine elements I 'll make a single, rare phenom-
      enon,
And of three common geniuses concoct a most uncom-
      mon one,
So that the world shall smile to see a soul so universal,
Such poesy and pleasantry, packed in so small a parcel."

So said, so done; the three in one she wrapped, and
      stuck the label:
Poet, Professor, Autocrat of Wit's own Breakfast-Table.

THE OLD MAN OF THE MOUNTAIN.[1]

ALL round the lake the wet woods shake
    From drooping boughs their showers of pearl ;
From floating skiff to towering cliff
    The rising vapors part and curl.
The west wind stirs among the firs
    High up the mountain side emerging ;
The light illumes a thousand plumes
    Through billowy banners round them surging.

A glory smites the craggy heights ;
    And in a halo of the haze,
Flushed with faint gold, far up, behold
    That mighty face, that stony gaze !

[1] Profile Notch, Franconia, N. H. The "Profile" is formed by separate projections of the cliff, which, viewed from a particular point, assume the marvelous appearance of a colossal human face.

7

In the wild sky upborne so high
  Above us perishable creatures,
Confronting Time with those sublime,
  Impassive, adamantine features.

Thou beaked and bald high front, miscalled
  The profile of a human face !
No kin art thou, O Titan brow,   ,
  To puny man's ephemeral race.
The groaning earth to thee gave birth,
  Throes and convulsions of the planet ;
Lonely uprose, in grand repose,
  Those eighty feet of facial granite.

Here long, while vast, slow ages passed,
  Thine eyes (if eyes be thine) beheld
But solitudes of crags and woods,
  Where eagles screamed and panthers yelled.
Before the fires of our pale sires
  In the first log-built cabin twinkled,
Or redmen came for fish and game,
  That scalp was scarred, that face was wrinkled.

We may not know how long ago
 That ancient countenance was young;
Thy sovereign brow was seamed as now
 When Moses wrote and Homer sung.
Empires and states it antedates,
 And wars, and arts, and crime, and glory;
In that dim morn when Christ was born
 Thy head with centuries was hoary.

Thou lonely one! nor frost, nor sun,
 Nor tempest leaves on thee its trace;
The stormy years are but as tears
 That pass from thy unchanging face.
With unconcern as grand and stern,
 Those features viewed, which now survey us,
A green world rise from seas of ice,·
 And order come from mud and chaos.

Canst thou not tell what then befell?
 What forces moved, or fast or slow;
How grew the hills; what heats, what chills,
 What strange, dim life, so long ago?

High-visaged peak, wilt thou not speak?
  One word, for all our learnèd wrangle !
What earthquakes shaped, what glaciers scraped,
  That nose, and gave the chin its angle?

Our pygmy thought to thee is naught,
  Our petty questionings are vain ;
In its great trance thy countenance
  Knows not compassion nor disdain.
With far-off hum we go and come,
  The gay, the grave, the busy-idle ;
And all things done to thee are one,
  Alike the burial and the bridal.

Thy permanence, long ages hence,
  Will mock the pride of mortals still.
Returning springs, with songs and wings
  And fragrance, shall these valleys fill ;
The free winds blow, fall rain or snow,
  The mountains brim their crystal beakers ;
Still come and go, still ebb and flow,
  The summer tides of pleasure-seekers : .

The dawns shall gild the peaks where build
   The eagles, many a future pair ;
The gray scud lag on wood and crag,
   Dissolving in the purple air ;
The sunlight gleam on lake and stream,
   Boughs wave, storms break, and still at even
All glorious hues the world suffuse,
   Heaven mantle earth, earth melt in heaven !

Nations shall pass like summer's grass,
   And times unborn grow old and change ;
New governments and great events
   Shall rise, and science new and strange ;
Yet will thy gaze confront the days
   With its eternal calm and patience,
The evening red still light thy head,
   Above thee burn the constellations.

O silent speech, that well can teach
   The little worth of words or fame !
I go my way, but thou wilt stay
   While future millions pass the same :

But what is this I seem to miss ?
  Those features fall into confusion !
A further pace — where was that face ?
  The veriest fugitive illusion !

Gray eidolon ! so quickly gone
  When eyes, that make thee, onward move ;
Whose vast pretense of permanence
  A little progress can disprove !
Like some huge wraith of human faith
  That to the mind takes form and measure ;
Grim monolith of creed or myth,
  Outlined against the eternal azure !

O Titan, how dislimned art thou !
  A withered cliff is all we see ;
That giant nose, that grand repose,
  Have in a moment ceased to be ;
Or still depend on lines that blend,
  On merging shapes, and sight, and distance,
And in the mind alone can find
  Imaginary brief existence !

UNDER MOON AND STARS.

FROM the house of desolation,
From the doors of lamentation,
I went forth into the midnight and the vistas of the
    moon ;
Where through aisles high-arched and shady
Paced the pale and spectral lady,
And with shining footprints silvered the deep velvet turf
    of June.

In the liquid hush and coolness
Of the slumbering earth, the fullness
Of my aching soul was solaced; till my senses, grown
    intense,
Caught the evanescent twinkle,
Caught the fairy-footed tinkle,
Of the dew-fall raining softly on the leafage cool and
    dense.

The sad cries, the unavailing

Orphans' tears and woman's wailing,

In the shuttered house were buried, and the pale face of

the dead ;

From the chambers closed and gloomy

Neither sight nor sound came to me,

But great silence was about me, and the great sky over-

head.

As a mighty angel leaneth

His calm visage from the zenith,

Gazed the moon : my thoughts flew upward, through the

pallid atmosphere,

To the planets in their places,

To the infinite starry spaces,

Till despair and death grew distant, and eternal Peace

drew near.

Then the faith that oft had failed me,

And the mad doubts that assailed me,

Like two armies that had struggled for some fortress long

and well,

Both as by a breath were banished ;
Friend and foe together vanished,
And my soul sat high and lonely in her solemn citadel.

Peace ! and from her starry station
Came white-pinioned Contemplation,
White and mystical and silent as the moonlight's sheeted
      wraith ;
Through my utter melancholy
Stole a rapture still and holy,
Something deeper than all doubting, something greater
      than all faith.

And I pondered : " Change is written
Over all the blue, star-litten
Universe ; the moon on high there, once a palpitating
      sphere,
Now is seamed with ghastly scissures,
Chilled and shrunken, cloven with fissures,
Sepulchres of frozen oceans and a perished atmosphere.

" Doubtless mid yon burning clusters
Ancient suns have paled their lustres,

Worlds are lost with all their wonders, glorious forms of
life and thought,
Arts and altars, lore of sages,
Monuments of mighty ages,
All that joyous nature lavished, all that toil and genius
wrought.

"So this dear, warm earth, and yonder
Sister worlds that with her wander
Round the parent light, shall perish ; on through darkening cycles run,
Whirling through their vast ellipses
Evermore in cold eclipses,
Orphaned planets roaming blindly round a cold and
darkened sun !

"This bright haze and exhalation,
Starry cloud we call creation,
Glittering mist of orbs and systems, shall like mist dissolve and fall, —
Seek the sea whence all ascendeth,
Meet the ocean where all endeth :
Thou alone art everlasting, O thou inmost Soul of all !

"Through all height, all depth, all distance,
    All duration, all existence,
Moves one universal nature, flows one vast Intelligence,
    Out of chaos and gray ruin
    Still the shining heavens renewing,
Flashing into light and beauty, flowering into form and
    sense.

"Veiled in manifold illusion,
    Seeming discord and confusion,
Life's harmonious scheme is builded : earth is but the
    outer stair,
    Is but scaffold-beam and stanchion
    In the rearing of the mansion.
Dust enfolds a finer substance, and the air, diviner air.

"All about the world and near it
    Lies the luminous realm of spirit,
Sometimes touching upturned foreheads with a strange,
    unearthly sheen ;
    Through the deep ethereal regions
    Throng invisible bright legions,
And unspeakable great glory flows around our lives un-
    seen ;

" Round our ignorance and anguish,
  Round the darkness where we languish,
As the sunlight round the dim earth's midnight tower of
  shadow pours,
  Streaming past the dim, wide portals,
  Viewless to the eyes of mortals
Till it flood the moon's pale islet or the morning's golden
  shores.

" Round the world of sense forever
  Rolls the bright, celestial river :
Of its presence, of its passing, streaks of faint prophetic
  light
  Give the mind mysterious warning,
  Gild its clouds with gleams of morning,
Or some shining soul reflects it to our feeble inner
  sight."

So by sheen and shade I wandered ;
And the mighty theme I pondered
(Vague and boundless as the midnight wrapping world
  and life and man)

Stooped with dewy whispers to me,
Breathed unuttered meanings through me,
Of man's petty pains and passions, of the grandeur of
God's plan !

And I said, "Thou one all-seeing,
Perfect, omnipresent Being,
Sparkling in the nearest dewdrop, throbbing in the far-
thest star ;
By the pulsing of whose power
Suns are sown and systems flower ;
Who hast called my soul from chaos and my faltering
feet thus far !

"What am I to make suggestion ?
What is man to doubt and question
Ways too wondrous for his searching, which no science
can reveal ?
Perfect and secure my trust is
In thy mercy and thy justice,
Though I perish as an insect by thine awful chariot-
wheel !

"Lo ! the shapes of ill and error,
Lo ! the forms of death and terror,
Are but light-obstructing phantoms, which shall vanish
late or soon,
Like this sudden, vast, appalling
Gloom on field and woodland falling
From the wingèd, black cloud-dragon that is flying by
the.moon ! "

Downward wheeled the dragon, driven
Like a falling fiend from heaven ;
And the silhouettes of the lindens, on the peaceful espla-
nade,
Lay once more like quiet islands
In the moonlight and the silence ;
And by softly silvered alleys, leafy mazes, still I strayed,

Till, through boughs of sombre maples,
With the pale gleam on its gables,
Lo ! the house of desolation, like a ghost amid the gloom !
Then the thought of present sorrow,
Of the palled, funereal morrow,
Filled anew my heart with anguish and the horror of the
tomb.

And I cried, " Is God above us ?
Are there Powers that guard and love us,
Pilots to the blissful havens ?   Do they hear the tones of
    woe,
Death and pain and separation,
Wailing through the wide creation ?
Will the high heavens heed or help us ; do they, can they
    feel and know ? "

Ah ! the heart is very human ;
Still the world of man and woman,
Love and loss, throbs in and through us !   For the radi-
    ant hour is rare,
When the soul from heights of vision
Views the shining plains Elysian,
And in after-times of trouble we forget what peace is
    there.

SONNETS.

I.

NATIVITY.

THISTLE and serpent we exterminate,
    Yet blame them not; and righteously abhor
    The crimes of men with all their kind at war,
Whom we may stay or slay, but not in hate.
By blood and brain we are predestinate
    Each to his course; and unawares therefor
    The heart's blind wish and inmost counselor
Makes times and tides; for man is his own fate.
Nativity is horoscope and star!
    One innocent egg incloses song and wings;
      One, deadly fangs and rattles set to warn.
Our days, our deeds, all we achieve or are,
    Lay folded in our infancy; the things
      Of good or ill we choose while yet unborn.

II.

CIRCUMSTANCE.

STALKING before the lords of life, one came,
  A Titan shape !   But often he will crawl,
  Their most subservient, helpful, humble thrall;
Swift as the light, or sluggish, laggard, lame;
Stony-eyed archer, launching without aim
  Arrows and lightnings, heedless how they fall, —
  Blind Circumstance, that makes or baffles all,
Happiness, length of days, power, riches, fame.
Could we but take each wingèd chance aright !
  A timely word let fall, a wind-blown germ,
    May crown our glebe with many a golden sheaf ;
A thought may touch and edge our life with light,
  Fill all its sphere, as yonder crescent worm
    Brightens upon the old moon's dusky leaf.

8

III.

PROVIDENCE.

WEARY with pondering many a weighty theme,
   I slept ; and in the realm of vision saw
   A mighty Angel reverently updraw
The cords of earth, all woven of gloom and gleam,
Wiles, woes, and many a silver-threaded stream
   Of sighs and prayers, and golden bands of law,
   And ties of faith and love, with many a flaw
Riven, but reunited in my dream.
These the great Angel, gathering, lifted high,
   Like mingled lines of rain and radiance, all
     In one bright, awful braid divinely blended,
That reached the beams of heaven, — a chain whereby
   This dimly glorious, shadow-brooding ball
     And home of man hung wondrously suspended.

THE TRAGEDY QUEEN.

HER triumphs are over, the crown
    Has passed from her brow ;
And she smiles, " To whom now does the town
    My poor laurels allow? "
It has wept for her, dying, a hundred times,
With mimic passion, in mimic crimes :
Who cares for her lying discrowned and dying
    In earnest now ?

Only those who have known her strange story,
    And watched her through all,
So serene in the day of her glory,
    So grand in her fall, —
In the sphere beyond all tragic art
Playing her own deep woman's part, —
A few faithful, befriend her, still cherish, attend her,
    And come at her call.

And so, when to-night the old fire
  Flamed up in her eye,
And she said, " 'T is a childish desire,
  I cannot deny,
To see the old boards and the footlights again,
To feel the wild storm of the plaudits of men !
But grant me this pastime, you know 't is the last time,"
  What could we reply ?

Her form to the carriage we bore
  In dark mantle and veil ;
On my arm, at the gloomy side-door,
  She hung, lily-like, frail ;
But, treading the old, familiar scene,
She moved majestic, she walked a queen —
The rouged ballet-girls staring to see her high bearing,
  So proud and so pale !

At the wing, her swift glance as we waited
  Swept royally round :
I could feel how she thrilled and dilated,
  And how at the sound,

The brief commotion that intervenes

, In the busy moment of shifting scenes,

The creaking of pulleys, the shrill shrieking *coulisse*,

  Her heart gave a bound.

  The manager hastes and unlocks

   The small door from the wing ;

  To the deep-curtained, crimson-lined box

   Our dear lady we bring.

All a-flutter with life, all a-glitter with light,

The vast half-circle burst on the sight ;

The fairy stage showing amidst, like a glowing

  Great gem in its ring.

  The strong soul in the weak woman's face

   Flashes forth to behold

  The gay world that assembled to grace

   Her own triumphs of old.

The vision brings back her bright young days —

For her the loud tumult, the showered bouquets ;

And her fancy is ravished with joy amid lavished

  Glory and gold.

In that moment of dream disappear
   Sorrow, sickness, and pain :
Airy hopes, a romantic career,
   Beam and beckon again.
Alas ! but the life itself could last
No more than the dream : and the dream is past —
'T is gone with the quickness of breath, while the sickness
   And sorrow remain.

We saw her, pain-stricken and white,
   Sink back in her place :
Could a pang of sharp envy so smite
   The brief joy from her face ?
Lo, the queen of the ballet ! she wavers and glides ;
Upon floods of strong music triumphant she rides,
And laughingly pillows each movement on billows
   Of beauty and grace.

And there, in his orchestra stall,
   The stage-vampire is seen,
Foremost once, most devoted of all,
   In the train of our queen.

Still seeking a fresh young heart to devour,
Still following ever the queen of the hour,
Enrapt by so rare a sight, sits the gray parasite,
    Ogling the scene.

    Not envy — her heart is too great.
      But for her, for all these,
    Whose fortunes, like flatterers, wait
      On their powers to please,
Whose unsubstantial happiness draws
Its air-plant life from the breath of applause,
The powers soon jaded, the flowers all faded
    And withered she sees ;

    The unworthy contentions, the strife ;
      Feet lured from the goals,
    Hands stayed in the contest of life,
      By the hour that cajoles
With its wayside-scattered apples of joy ;
The sunshine that pampers, the storms that destroy,
And all the besetting temptations benetting
    These butterfly souls.

And naught, as we know, can assuage
   Her keen anguish of heart,
Seeing thus from her dearly loved stage
   The true grandeur depart.
Now the people prefer these wonder-shows,
Scant costume, antics and flushed tableaux ;
For tinsel and magic, forgetting her tragic
   Magnificent art.

"Let us go ! " she entreats ; " I am ill ! "
   And unnoticed withdraws
From the theatre, thundering still
   With the surge of applause.
As slowly she turns behind the scene
For a parting glance, comes the gay new queen,
By fairies attended, all glowing and splendid
   In spangles and gauze.

From the footlights, arms filled with bouquets,
   One is hurrying back ;
One gazes with cold marble face
   From the veil's tragic black :

And there at the manager's beck they meet ;
The new queen stoops at the old queen's feet,
With all her soft graces, and sweet commonplaces
    Of greeting no lack.

    Before her the great lady stood,
      So gracious, so grand !
  " You are lovely — I think you are good :
      O child, understand !
Be prudent, yet generous ; false to none ;
Keep the pearl of the heart ; be true to one ;
Be wise, oh, be gentle ! " and from the dark mantle
    She reached forth her hand.

    And they parted.   All freshness and fire,
      One passed in her bloom,
    Feet swift with delight and desire,
      Arms shedding perfume !
From the cold dim coach one looks her last
At the theatre lights and the joyous past,
As away in the lurid wet night we are hurried,
    Through rain-gust and gloom.

THE OLD LOBSTERMAN.

CAPE ARUNDEL, KENNEBUNKPORT, MAINE.

Just back from a beach of sand and shells,
  And shingle the tides leave oozy and dank,
Summer and winter the old man dwells
  In his low brown house on the river bank.
Tempest and sea-fog sweep the hoar
And wrinkled sand-drifts round his door,
Where often I see him sit, as gray
And weather-beaten and lonely as they.

Coarse grasses wave on the arid swells
  In the wind ; and two bright poplar-trees
Seem hung all over with silver bells
  That tinkle and twinkle in sun and breeze.
All else is desolate sand and stone :
And here the old lobsterman lives alone :

Nor other companionship has he
But to sit in his house and gaze at the sea.

A furlong or more away to the south,
　On the bar beyond the huge sea-walls
That keep the channel and guard its mouth,
　The high, curved billow whitens and falls ;
And the racing tides through the granite gate,
On their wild errands that will not wait,
Forever, unresting, to and fro,
Course with impetuous ebb and flow.

They bury the barnacled ledge, and make
　Into every inlet and crooked creek,
And flood the flats with a shining lake,
　Which the proud ship plows with foam at her beak :
The ships go up to yonder town,
Or over the sea their hulls sink down,
And many a pleasure pinnace rides
On the restless backs of the rushing tides.

I try to fathom the gazer's dreams,
　But little I gain from his gruff replies ;

Far off, far off the spirit seems,
   As he looks at me with those strange gray eyes;
Never a hail from the shipwrecked heart !
Mysterious oceans seem to part
The desolate man from all his kind —
The Selkirk of his lonely mind.

He has growls for me when I bring him back
   My unused bait — his way to thank;
And a good shrill curse for the fishing-smack
   That jams his dory against the bank;
But never a word of love to give
For love, — ah ! how can he bear to live ?
I marvel, and make my own heart ache
With thinking how his must sometimes break.

Solace he finds in the sea, no doubt.
   To catch the ebb he is up and away.
I see him silently pushing out
   On the broad bright gleam at break of day;
And watch his lessening dory toss
On the purple crests as he pulls across,
Round reefs where silvery surges leap,
And meets the dawn on the rosy deep.

His soul, is it open to sea and sky?
   His spirit, alive to sound and sight?
What wondrous tints on the water lie —
   Wild, wavering, liquid realm of light !
Between two glories looms the shape
Of the wood-crested, cool green cape,
Sloping all round to foam-laced ledge,
And cavern and cove, at the bright sea's edge.

He makes for the floats that mark the spots,
   And rises and falls on the sweeping swells,
Ships oars, and pulls his lobster-pots,
   And tumbles the tangled claws and shells
In the leaky bottom ; and bails his skiff ;
While the slow waves thunder along the cliff,
And foam far away where sun and mist
Edge all the region with amethyst.

I watch him, and fancy how, a boy,
   Round these same reefs, in the rising sun,
He rowed and rocked, and shouted for joy,
   As over the boat-side one by one

He lifted and launched his lobster-traps,
And reckoned his gains, and dreamed, perhaps,
Of a future as glorious, vast and bright
As the ocean, unrolled in the morning light.

He quitted his skiff for a merchant-ship;
   Was sailor-boy, mate, — gained skill and command;
And brought home once from a fortunate trip
   A wife he had found in a foreign land:
So the story is told: then settled down
With the nabobs of his native town, —
Jolly old skippers, bluff and hale,
Who owned the bottoms they used to sail.

Does he sometimes now, in his loneliness,
   Live over again that happy time,
Beguile his poverty and distress
   With pictures of his prosperous prime?
Does ever, at dusk, a fond young bride
Start forth and sit by the old man's side;
Children frolic, and friends look in;
With all the blessings that might have been?

Yet might not be !   The same sad day
   Saw wife and babe to the churchyard borne ;
And he sailed away, he sailed away, —
   For that is the sailor's way to mourn.
And ever, 't is said, as he sailed and sailed,
Heart grew reckless and fortune failed,
Till old age drifted him back to shore,
To his hut and his lobster-pots once more.

The house is empty, the board is bare ;
   His dish he scours, his jacket he mends ;
And now 't is the dory that needs repair ;
   He fishes ; his lobster-traps he tends ;
And, rowing at nightfall many a mile,
Brings floodwood home to his winter pile ;
Then his fire 's to kindle, and supper to cook ;
The storm his music, his thoughts his book.

He sleeps, he wakes ; and this is his life.
   Nor kindred nor friend in all the earth ;
Nor laughter of child, nor gossip of wife ;
   Not even a cat to his silent hearth !

Only the sand-hills, wrinkled and hoar,
Bask in the sunset, round his door,
Where now I can see him sit, as gray
And weather-beaten and lonely as they.

OLD MAN GRAM.

In little Gram Court lives old man Gram,
    The patriarch of the place ;
    Where often you 'll see his face,
Eager and greedy, peering about,
As he goes bustling in and out,
    At a wriggling, rickety pace,
    Brisk octogenarian's pace.
He rattles his stick at my heels, and brags
As he comes shuffling along the flags,
Brags of his riches and brags of his rags,
    Much work and little play.
"You see where I am," says old man Gram,
    "You see where I am to-day !

"I came to town at twelve years old,
    With a shilling in this 'ere pocket," —
    You should see him chuckle and knock it !

9

" The town to me was a big stout chest,
  With fortunes locked in the till, but I guessed
      A silver key would unlock it,
      My little key would unlock it !
I found in a rag-shop kept by a Jew
A place to sleep and a job to do,
And managed to make my shilling two ;
      And that 's always been my way.
Now see where I am," cries old man Gram,
      " Now see where I am to-day ! "

In his den a-top of the butcher's shop,
      He lies in his lair of husks,
      And sups on gruels and rusks,
And a bone now and then, to pick and gnaw,
With hardly a tooth in his tough old jaw,
      But a couple of curious tusks,
      Ah, picturesque, terrible tusks !
Though half Gram Court he calls his own,
Here, hoarding his rents, he has lived alone,
Until, like a hungry wolf, he has grown
      Gaunt and shaggy and gray.
  " You see where I am," growled old man Gram,
      As I looked in to-day.

" I might have a wife to make my broth, —

    Which would be convenient, rather !

    And younkers to call me father ;

But a wife would be after my chink, you see,

And — bantlings for them that like ! " snarls he ;

    " I never would have the bother ;

    They 're an awful expense and bother !

I went to propose at fifty-four,

But stopped as I raised my hand to the door ;

' To think of a dozen brats or more ! '

    Says I, and I turned away.

Now see where I am," brags old man Gram,

    " Only see where I am to-day !

" I had once a niece, who came to town

    As poor as any church mouse ;

    She wanted to keep my house !

' Tut ! I have no house to keep ! go back ! '

I gave her a dollar and told her to pack ;

    At which she made such a touse —

    You never did see such a touse !

Whole rows of houses were mine, she said ;

I had more bank shares than hairs in my head,

And gold like so much iron or lead —
    All which I could n't gainsay.
Men see where I am," grins old man Gram;
    " They see where I am to-day.

" But if there is anything I detest,
        And for which I have no occasion,
        Sir, it 's a poor relation !
They 're always plenty, and always in need ;
Take one, and soon you will have to feed
        Just about half the nation ;
        They 'll swarm from all over the nation !
And I have a rule, though it 's nothing new :
'T is a lesson I learned from my friend, the Jew :
Whatever I fancy, whatever I do,
        I always ask, Will it pay ?
Now see where I am," boasts old man Gram,
    " Just see where I am to-day ! "

The little boys dread his coming tread,
        They are pale as he passes by ;
        And the sauciest curs are shy, —

His stick is so thick, and he looks so grim ;
Not even a beggar will beg of him,
 You should hear him mention why !
 There 's a very good reason why.
The poor he hates, and he has n't a friend,
And none but a fool will give or lend ;
" For, only begin, there 'll be no end ;
 That 's what I always say.
Now see where I am," crows old man **Gram**,
 " Just see where I am to-day ! "

His miserly gain is the harvest-grain,
 All the rest is chaff and stubble ;
 And the life beyond is a bubble :
We are as the beasts : and he thinks, on the whole,
It 's quite as well that he has no soul,
 For that might give him trouble,
 Might give him a deal of trouble !
The long and short of the old man's creed,
Is to live for himself and to feed his greed :
The world is a very good world indeed,
 If only a chap might stay ;
" Only stay where I am," whines old man **Gram**,
 " Stay just where I am to-day ! "

THE ISLE OF LAMBS.

In sunlight slept the gilded cliff,
    The ocean beat below,
The gray gulls flapped along the wave,
    The seas broke, huge and slow.

The drenched rocks rose like buffaloes,
    With matted sea-weed manes ;
Each shaggy hide shook off the tide
    In dripping crystal rains.

Up rose Monk Rock's bald scalp and locks :
    The heavy, drownèd hair
Below the crown hung sad and brown,
    The crown was bleached and bare.

And out from shore, a league or more,
    Entranced in purple calms,

Where summer seemed eternal, dreamed
　　The lovely Isle of Lambs.

I said : " Those rocks like scattered flocks
　　Lie basking in the sun,
And fancy sees a golden fleece
　　Enfolding every one."

An old man sat upon the cliff ;
　　His hair like silver flame
Flared in the breeze : " Not so," he said,
　　" Our island got its name.

" But as each year our sheep we shear,
　　The younglings of the flock
Are chosen, and banished to that small
　　Green world of grass and rock.

" There, pastured on the virgin turf,
　　And watered faithfully
By rain and dew, the summer through,
　　Encircled by the sea,

"They sport, they lie beneath the sky,
　　Fenced in by shining waves,
　Or shelter seek, when winds are bleak,
　　Among the cliffs and caves."

Still as I questioned him, he said :
　　"This quiet farm I till."
A house he showed high up the road,
　　Half hidden by the hill.

"'Tis now threescore long years and more,
　　Long years of lonely toil,
　Since Ruth and I came here, to try
　　Our fortunes on the soil.

"Not yet for me God's sun had risen,
　　His face I could not see ;
　But she, my light, my moon by night,
　　Reflected Him to me.

"So when she died my world was dark ;
　　No hope, but grim Despair,
　Despair and Hate, his gloomy mate,
　　Walked with me everywhere.

" They laid their burden on my soul ;
 They would not let me pray ;
Hate and Despair, a dismal pair,
 Were with me night and day.

" They said : ' Behold the fisher-boy !
 He laughs a lengthened peal.
For bait he takes a worm, or breaks
 The cockle with his heel ;

" ' Nor heeds the whitening barnacles,
 As crushingly he tramps
By the sea's edge, along the ledge
 Encrusted with their camps.'

" Then I beheld the living fish
 Their small companions slay,
And barnacles, in rocky wells,
 That snatched a viewless prey.

" The barnacles, fine fishermen,
 Their tiny scoop-nets swung ;
Each breathing shell within the well
 Shot forth a shadowy tongue.

" Then said Despair : 'So all things fare ;
    Alike the great and small.'
Then muttered Hate : ' Yea, God is great !
    He preyeth upon all ! '

" So shearing-time came round again ;
    And when my sheep were shorn,
Beneath the cliff I rigged my skiff,
    One pleasant summer morn.

" The stars were gone ; I saw the Dawn
    Her crown of glory lay
With misty smile on yonder isle,
    And something seemed to say :

" ' Who spread those pastures for thy flock ?
    Who sends the herb and dew ?
Who curved round all this crystal wall ?
    He is thy Shepherd, too ! '

" Windrows of kelp lay on the beach,
    Sent hither by the storm ;
The sea's rich spoil, our meagre soil
    To nourish and to warm.

" Against the course of winds and foam,
　Shoreward, from steadfast deeps,
With mighty flow the undertow
　Its rolling burden sweeps.

" And something whispered in my heart :
　' Beneath the waves of wrong,
The surface flow of wrong and woe,
　Are currents deep and strong,

" ' Unseen, that still to those who wait
　Bring blessedness and help.'
But, dark and stern, I would not learn
　The lesson of the kelp.

" The lambs were bound, and one by one
　I took them from the sand,
Till, all afloat in my good boat,
　I pushed out from the land.

" I took the oar, I pushed from shore ;
　And then I smiled to see ．
One poor, scared thing upstart and spring,
　His fettered limbs to free.

" 'You foolish lamb ! ' I chided him,
   ' Have faith in me and wait.
  You do but gain a needless pain
   By striving with your fate.

" 'I know your grief, the end I know.
   Those hazy slopes, that rise
  From out the sea, to you shall be
   A summer paradise.'

" The light oars dipped, they rose and dripped,
   The ripples ran beneath,
  In many a whirl of pink and pearl,
   In many a sparkling wreath.

" With long, smooth swell arose and fell
   The slow, uncertain seas,
  Till something stole into my soul
   Of their soft light and peace.

" A flush of hope, a breath of joy,
   To know that still for me
  The dawn's bright hues could so suffuse
   That pure translucency.

" But, when the voyage was almost done,
　　The discontented lamb,
　With one glad bleat, shook free his feet,
　　Leaped from the skiff, and swam.

" Far off the tall, forbidding wall
　　Of rocky coast was seen ;
　The sea was cold, the billows rolled
　　A restless host between.

" Billows before and all around —
　　A billowy world to swim ;
　Only the boat was there afloat
　　On the wide waves with him.

" He turned, dismayed ; but looked in vain
　　His following mates to see ;
　All, snug and warm and safe from harm,
　　Were in the skiff with me.

" Ah ! then he knew his shepherd's voice !
　　With cries of quick distress,
　Straight to my beckoning hand he came,
　　In utter helplessness.

"With piteous cries, with pleading eyes,
        Upon my friendly palm
    He stretched his chin; I drew him in,
        A chilled and dripping lamb.

"'This poor, repentant beast,' I said,
        'Is wiser far than I ;
    Against God's will rebellious still,
        I beat the waves and cry.

"'O Love look down ! I sink ! I drown !
        Is there no hand to reach
    A pleading soul ? ' My boat, meanwhile,
        Drew near the rocky beach.

"How calm the waves ! How clear the sea !
        Mysterious and slow,
    In that deep glass, the long eel-grass
        Went waving to and fro.

"Safely to shore my freight I bore ;
        Their morning voyage was done.
    I loosed their bands upon the sands
        And freed them, one by one.

" They climbed the fresh and dewy slopes,
    They wandered everywhere ;
With many a sweet and gladsome bleat,
    They blessed the island air.

" The beach-birds ran among the rocks,
    And, like an infant's hand,
A little star-fish stretched its five
    Pink fingers on the sand.

" Invisible, on some high crest,
    One solitary bird
Trilled clear and strong his morning song,
    The sweetest ever heard.

" The sky, all light and love, looked down
    Upon the curtained sea ;
The dimpled deep in rosy sleep
    Lay breathing tranquilly.

" Upon the island's topmost rock
    I basked in holy calms ;
My proud heart there I bowed in prayer,
    My joy broke forth in psalms.

"O stranger! you are young, and I
　　Am in the shadowy vale ;
Fourscore and ten the years have been
　　Of him who tells this tale.

" And do you marvel at the peace
　　That goes with hoary hairs,
This heritage of blessed age
　　Which my glad spirit bears ?

" The secret is not far to seek,
　　If you can tell me why
One lamb thenceforth, of all my flock,
　　Was precious in my eye ;

" And wherefore he, more faithfully
　　And fondly than the rest,
Learned to obey my voice and lay
　　His head upon my breast."

That old man rose, he passed away
　　In sunshine soft and still,
To his abode, high up the road,
　　Behind the sunlit hill.

Then half I thought, such peace he brought,
  So clothed in light was he,
That on that coast a heavenly ghost
  Had met and talked with me.

    10

THE BOY I LOVE.

My boy, do you know the boy I love?
    I fancy I see him now;
His forehead bare in the sweet spring air,
With the wind of hope in his waving hair,
    The sunrise on his brow.

He is something near your height, may be;
    And just about your years;
Timid as you; but his will is strong,
And his love of right and his hate of wrong
    Are mightier than his fears.

He has the courage of simple truth.
    The trial that he must bear,
The peril, the ghost that frights him most,
He faces boldly, and like a ghost
    It vanishes in air.

As wildfowl take, by river and lake,
　　The sunshine and the rain,
With cheerful, constant hardihood
He meets the bad luck and the good,
　　The pleasure and the pain.

Come friends in need?　With heart and deed
　　He gives himself to them.
He has the grace which reverence lends, —
Reverence, the crowning flower that bends
　　The upright lily-stem.

Though deep and strong his sense of wrong,
　　Fiery his blood and young,
His spirit is gentle, his heart is great,
He is swift to pardon and slow to hate,
　　And master of his tongue.

Fond of his sports?　No merrier lad's
　　Sweet laughter ever rang!
But he is so generous and so frank,
His wildest wit or his maddest prank
　　Can never cause a pang.

His own sweet ease, all things that please,
    He loves, like any boy;
But fosters a prudent fortitude;
Nor will he squander a future good
    To buy a fleeting joy.

Face brown or fair?   I little care,
    Whatever the hue may be,
Or whether his eyes are dark or light;
If his tongue be true and his honor bright,
    He is still the boy for me.

Where does he dwell?   I cannot tell;
    Nor do I know his name.
Or poor, or rich?   I don't mind which;
Or learning Latin, or digging ditch;
    I love him all the same.

With high, brave heart perform your part,
    Be noble and kind as he,
Then, some fair morning, when you pass,
Fresh from glad dreams, before your glass,
    His likeness you may see.

You are puzzled ?   What ! you think there is not
    A boy like him, — surmise
That he is only a bright ideal ?
But you have power to make him real,
    And clothe him to our eyes.

You have rightly guessed : in each pure breast
    Is his abiding-place.
Then let your own true life portray
His beauty, and blossom day by day
    With something of his grace.

ANCESTORS.

OPEN lies the book before me : in a realm obscure as
    dreams
I can trace the pale blue mazes of innumerable streams,
That from regions lost in distance, vales of shadow far
    apart,
Meet to blend their mystic forces in the torrents of my
    heart.

Pensively I turn the pages, pausing, curious and aghast :
What commingled, unknown currents, mighty passions of
    the past,
In this narrow, pulsing moment through my fragile being
    pour,
From the mystery behind me, to the mystery before !

I put by the book : in vision rise the gray ancestral
    ghosts,

Reaching back into the ages, vague, interminable hosts,

From the home of modern culture, to the cave uncouth
    and dim,

Where — what 's he that gropes? a savage, naked, gib-
    bering, and grim !

I was molded in that far-off time of ignorance and wrong,

When the world was to the crafty, to the ravenous and
    strong ;

Tempered in the fires of struggle, of aggression and re-
    sistance :

In the prowler and the slayer I have had a preëxistence !

Wild forefathers, I salute you !   Though your times were
    fierce and rude,

From their rugged husk of evil comes the kernel of our
    good.

Sweet the righteousness that follows, great the forces
    that foreran :

'T is the marvel still of marvels that there 's such a thing
    as man !

Now I see I have exacted too much justice of my race,

Of my own heart too much wisdom, of my brothers too
much grace ;

Craft and greed our primal dower, wrath and hate our
heritage !

Scarcely gleams as yet the crescent of the full-orbed
golden age.

Man's great passions are coeval with the vital breath he
draws,

Older than all codes of custom, all religions and all laws ;

Before prudence was, or justice, they were proved and
justified :

We may shame them and deny them, their dominion will
abide.

Still the darker age will linger in the slowly brightening
present,

Still the old moon's fading phantom in the bosom of the
crescent ;

The white crown of reason covers the old kingdom of
unrest,

And I feel at times the stirring of the savage in my
breast.

Wrong and insult find me weaponed for a more heroic
      strife ;

In the sheath of mercy quivers the barbarian's ready
      knife !

But I blame no more the givers for the rudeness of the
      dower :

'T was the roughness of the thistle that insured the future
      flower.

Somehow hidden in the slayer was the singer yet to be,

In the fiercest of my fathers lived the prophecy of me ;

But the turbid rivers flowing to my heart were filtered
      through

Tranquil veins of honest toilers to a more cerulean hue.

O my fathers, in whose bosoms slowly dawned the later
      light,

In whom grew the thirst for knowledge, in whom burned
      the love of right,

All my heart goes out to know you ! With a yearning
      near to pain,

I once more take up the volume, but I turn the leaves in
      vain.

Not a voice, of all your voices, comes to me from out the
    vast;
Not a thought, of all your thinking, into living form has
    passed:
As I peer into the darkness, not a being of my name
Stands revealed against the shadows in the beacon-glare
    of fame.

Yet your presence, O my parents, in my inmost self I
    find,
Your persistent spectres haunting the dim chambers of
    the mind:
Old convulsions of the planet in the new earth leave
    their trace,
And the child's heart is an index to the story of his
    race.

Each with his unuttered secret down the common road
    you went,
Winged with hope and exultation, bowed with toil and
    discontent:
Fear and triumph and bereavement, birth and death and
    love and strife,
Wove the evanescent vesture of your many-colored life.

Your long-silent generations first in me have found a
    tongue,

And I bear the mystic burden of a thousand lives un-
    sung :

Hence this love for all that 's human, the strange sym-
    pathies I feel,

Subtle memories and emotions which I stammer to re-
    veal.

Now I also, in my season, walk beneath the sun and
    moon,

Face the hoary storms of winter, breathe the luxury of
    June :

Here to gaze awhile and wonder, here to weep and laugh
    and kiss ;

Then to join the pale procession sweeping down the
    dark abyss.

To each little life its moment ! We are sparkles of the
    sea :

Still the interminable billows heave and gleam, — and
    where are we ?

Still forever rising, following, mingling with the mighty
    roar,
Wave on wave the generations break upon the eternal
    shore.

Here I joy and sing and suffer, in this moment fleeting
    fast,
Then become myself a phantom of the far-receding past,
When our modern shall be ancient, and the narrow times
    expand,
Down through ever-broadening eras, to a future vast and
    grand.

Clouds of ancestors, ascending from this sublunary coast,
Here am I, enrolled already in your ever-mustering host !
Here and now the rivers blended in my blood once more
    divide,
In the fair lad leaping yonder, in these darlings by my
    side.

Children's children, I salute you ! From this hour and
    from this land,
To your far off generations I uplift the signal hand !

Well contented, I resign you to the vision which I see, —
O fraternity of nations! O republics yet to be!

Yours the full-blown flower of freedom, which in struggle
    we have sown;
Yours the spiritual science, that shall overarch our own.
You, in turn, will look with wonder, from a more enlight-
    ened time,
Upon us, your rude forefathers, in an age of war and
    crime!

Half our virtues will seem vices by your broader, higher
    right,
And the brightness of the present will be shadow in that
    light;
For, behold, our boasted culture is a morning cloud, un-
    furled
In the dawning of the ages and the twilight of the world!

TWOSCORE AND TEN.

ACROSS the sleepy, sun-barred atmosphere
 Of the pew-checkered, square old meeting-house,
Through the high window, I could see and hear
 The far crows cawing in the forest boughs.

The earnest preacher talked of Youth and Age :
 " Life is a book, whose lines are flitting fast ;
Each word a moment, every year a page,
 Till, leaf by leaf, we quickly turn the last."

Even while he spoke, the sunshine's witness crept
 By many a fair and many a grizzled head,
Some drooping heavily, as if they slept,
 Over the unspelled minutes as they sped.

A boy of twelve, with fancies fresh and strong,
 Who found the text no cushion of repose,

Who deemed the shortest sermon far too long,
    My thoughts were in the tree-tops with the crows ;

Or farther still I soared, upon the back
    Of white clouds sailing in the shoreless blue,
Till he recalled me from their dazzling track
    To the old meeting-house and high-backed pew.

" *To eager childhood, as it turns the leaf,*
    How long and bright the unread page appears !
But to the aged, looking back, how brief,
    How brief the tale of half a hundred years !"

Over the drowsy pews the preacher's word
    Resounded, as he paused to wipe his brows :
I seem to hear it now, as then I heard,
    Reëchoing in the hollow meeting-house.

" *Our youth is gone, and thick and thicker come*
    The hoary years, like tempest-driven snows ;
Flies fast, flies fast, life's wasting pendulum,
    And ever faster as it shorter grows."

My mates sat wondering wearily the while
How long before his *Lastly* would come in,
Or glancing at the girls across the aisle,
Or in some distant corner playing pin.

But in that moment to my inward eyes
A sudden window opened, and I caught
Through dazzling rifts a glimpse of other skies,
The dizzy deeps, the blue abyss of thought.

Beside me sat my father, grave and gray,
And old, so old, at twoscore years and ten !
I said, " I will remember him this day,
When *I* am fifty, if I live till then.

" I will remember all I see and hear,
My very thoughts, and how life seems to me,
This Sunday morning in my thirteenth year ; —
How will it seem when I am old as he ?

" What is the work that I shall find to do ?
Shall I be worthy of his honored name ?

Poor and obscure ? or will my dream come true,
 My secret dream of happiness and fame ? "

Ah me, the years betwixt that hour and this !
 The ancient meeting-house has passed away,
And in its place a modern edifice
 Invites the well-dressed worshiper to-day.

With it have passed the well-remembered faces :
 The old are gone, the boys are gray-haired men ;
They too are scattered, strangers fill their places ;
 And here am I at twoscore years and ten !

How strangely, wandering here beside the-sea,
 The voice of crows in yonder forest boughs,
A cloud, a Sabbath bell, bring back to me
 That morning in the gaunt old meeting-house !

An oasis amid the desert years,
 That golden Sunday smiles as then it smiled :
I see the venerated head ; through tears
 I see myself, that far-off wondering child !

11

The pews, the preacher, and the whitewashed wall,
　An imaged book, with careless children turning
Its awful pages, — I remember all ;
　My very thoughts, the questioning and yearning ;

The haunting faith, the shadowy superstition,
　That I was somehow chosen, the special care
Of Powers that led me through life's changeful vision,
　Spirits and Influences of earth and air.

In curious pity of myself, grown wise,
　I think what then I was and dared to hope,
And how my poor achievements satirize
　The boy's brave dream and happy horoscope.

To see the future flushed with morning fire,
　Rosy with banners, bright with beckoning spears,
Fresh fields inviting courage and desire, —
　This is the glory of our youthful years.

To feel the pettiness of prizes won,
　With all our vast ambition ; to behold
So much attempted and so little done, —
　This is the bitterness of growing old.

Yet why repine ?   Though soon we care no more
   For triumphs which, till won, appear so sweet,
They serve their use, as toys held out before
   Beguiled our infancy to try its feet.

Not in rewards, but in the strength to strive,
   The blessing lies, and new experience gained ;
In daily duties done, hope kept alive,
   That Love and Thought are housed and entertained.

So not in vain the struggle, though the prize
   Awaiting me was other than it seemed.
My feet have missed the paths of Paradise,
   Yet life is even more blessed than I deemed.

Riches I never sought, and have not found,
   And Fame has passed me with averted eye ;
In creeks and bays my quiet voyage is bound,
   While the great world without goes surging by.

No withering envy of another's lot,
   Nor nightmare of contention, plagues my rest :
For me alike what is and what is not,
   Both what I have and what I lack, are best.

A flower more sacred than far-seén success
    Perfumes my solitary path ; I find
Sweet compensation in my humbleness,
    And reap the harvest of a tranquil mind.

I keep some portion of my early dream :
    Brokenly bright, like moonbeams on a river,
It lights my life, a far elusive gleam,
    Moves as I move, and leads me on forever.

Our earliest longings prophesy the man,
    Our fullest wisdom still enfolds the child ;
And in my life I trace that larger plan
    Whereby at last all things are reconciled.

The storm-clad years, the years that howl ánd hasten,
    The world, where simple faith soon grows estranged,
Toil, passion, loss, all things that mold and chasten,
    Still leave the inmost part of us unchanged.

O boy of long ago, whose name I bear,
    Small self, half-hidden by the antique pew,
Across the years I see you, sitting there,
    Wondering and gazing out into the blue ;

And marvel at this sober, gray-haired man
   I am or seem !   How changed my days, how tame
The wild, swift hopes with which my youth began !
   Yet in my inmost self I am the same.

The dreamy soul, too sensitive and shy,
   The brooding tenderness for bird and flower
The old, old wonder at the earth and sky,
   And sense of guidance by an Unseen Power, —

These keep perpetual childhood in my heart.
   The peaks of age, that looked so bare and cold,
Those peaks and I are still as far apart
   As in the years when fifty seemed so old.

Age, that appeared far off a bourn at rest,
   Recedes as I advance ; the fount of joy
Rises perennial in my grateful breast ;
   And still at fifty I am but a boy.

THE END.